Dear Little Lamb,

By Christa Kempter
Illustrated by Frauke Weldin

Translated by Michelle Maczka

NORTHSOUTH
BOOKS
New York / London

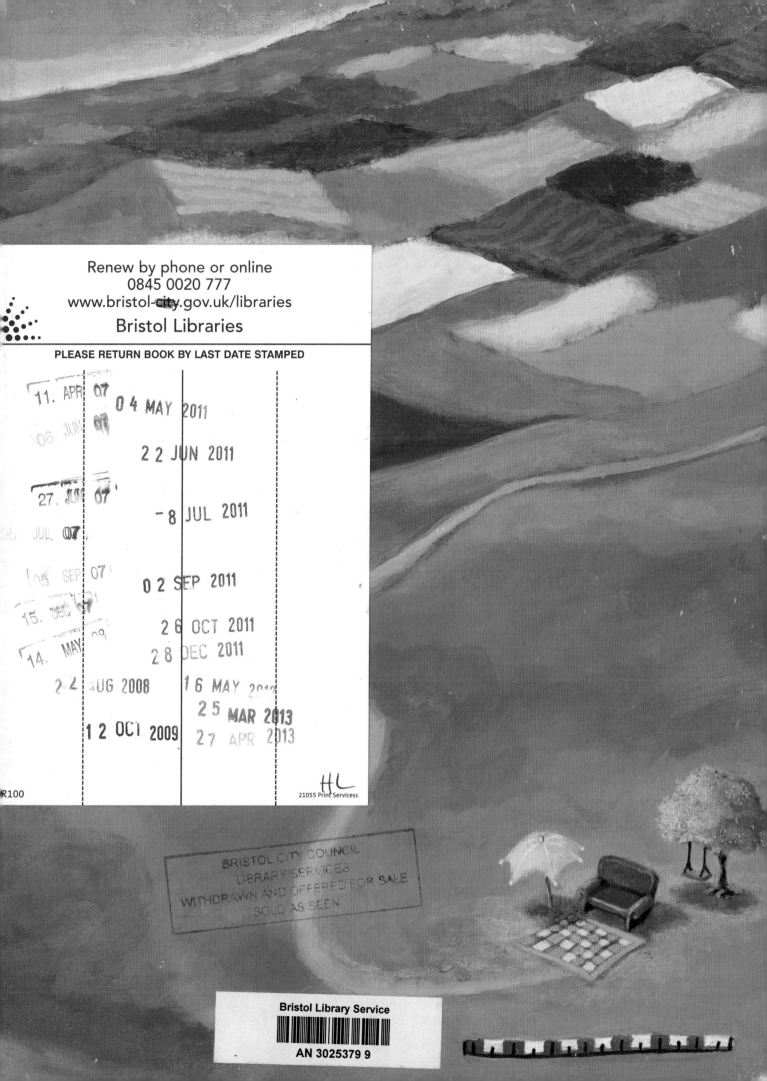

Copyright © 2006 by NordSüd Verlag AG, Gossau Zürich, Switzerland
First published in Switzerland under the title *Liebes kleines Schaf*

English translation copyright © 2006 by North-South Books Inc., New York.

First published in the United States, Great Britain, Canada, Australia, and
New Zealand in 2006 by North-South Books Inc., an imprint of
NordSüd Verlag AG, Gossau Zürich, Switzerland. Distributed in
the United States by North-South Books Inc., New York.

Library of Congress Cataloging-in-Publication Data is available.
A CIP catalogue record for this book is available from The British Library.

ISBN-13: 978-0-7358-2086-9 / ISBN-10: 0-7358-2086-4 (trade edition)
10 9 8 7 6 5 4 3 2 1

Printed in Belgium

Wolf stood high on the mountain, peering through his telescope at the valley below. And what did he see? A small, white, fluffy thing was leaping about in the green meadow.

"Yum, yum." Wolf drooled. "I'm going to catch that fluffy Little Lamb!"

But the valley was far away, and the wolf wasn't that young anymore.

So Wolf sat down to write a letter. A clever beginning is best, he thought.

Dear Little Lamb,

   I live far away, but I saw you through my telescope
and you look very nice.
   Won't you be my friend? I'm really very lonely.
Please write back soon.

Your friend,
Wolfgang

P.S. If you could, please put a small sausage in
the envelope when you write back to me.

The post office was halfway down the mountain. Wolf went there early every morning to pick up the *Wolf Times* because there was no mail carrier to deliver it.

An old, gray dog sat behind the counter. He was eating a nice, juicy sausage as Wolf entered, flinging down the letter for Little Lamb. The dog picked up his magnifying glass and read the envelope.

"Which lamb is this for? There are a number of little lambs," he muttered.

"But only one that's so small, tender, and fluffy," snarled Wolf, snatching the sausage right off the old, gray dog's plate and gobbling it up.

Every afternoon, Papa Sheep went to the post office to pick up the *Sheep News.*

"Oh, by the way, there's a letter here for a small, tender, fluffy Little Lamb," muttered the old, gray dog. "Do you know who it could be?"

"Why, that has to be our child!" said Papa Sheep happily.

"Is he small, tender, and fluffy?"

"Of course," declared Papa Sheep.

"All right then," grumbled the old, gray dog, handing Papa Sheep the letter.

"You got a letter, Little Lamb!" cried Papa Sheep.

"For me?" asked Little Lamb excitedly.

Papa Sheep read the letter out loud.

Little Lamb was delighted. "Wow, I've always wanted a friend!" He dictated a letter to Papa Sheep at once.

Dear Wolfgang,

I'm so happy to finally have a friend. Too bad you live so far away.

I understand the part about the telescope. But I don't get the bit about the sausage. Sheep don't eat sausages! My papa makes a tasty cabbage soup though, in case you want to visit me sometime.

Your friend,
Little Lamb

Mama Sheep shook her head in astonishment.

The days passed and the letters went back and forth. Each morning, Wolf picked up his newspaper and mail, and brought another letter for Little Lamb. Every afternoon, Papa Sheep picked up his newspaper and mail, and brought another letter for Wolf. For the last week, Wolf had eaten nothing but pancakes.

It's about time that I ate that Little Lamb, he thought, and wrote:

Dear Little Lamb,

Don't you think we should meet? How about this Sunday, at eleven o'clock, behind the post office? If you'll come, I'll tell you lots of stories about the many delicious sheep that live in Australia and about the especially tender grass there.

Your friend,
Wolfgang

Mama Sheep read this letter out loud to Little Lamb. "My darling, it's out of the question. I want to take a good look at this Wolfgang first," she said.

"But he's my friend!" cried Little Lamb defiantly and stomped his foot.

But Mama Sheep was suspicious. That line in the letter about "*delicious* sheep" made her distinctly uncomfortable.

On Sunday morning, Mama Sheep stormed over to the post office.

"What are you so angry about?" muttered the old, gray dog. "I don't even know you!"

"I am Mama Sheep, Little Lamb's mother and Papa Sheep's wife. Is that clear?"

"Perfectly," muttered the old, gray dog.

"Who's this Wolfgang who keeps writing to our child?" asked Mama Sheep.

"Sorry. I can't reveal that information. Postal rules, you know," whispered the old, gray dog.

"Then I'll just wait for him," huffed Mama Sheep.

It wasn't long before Wolf stormed up to the post office. "Is there a letter for me from Little Lamb?" he shouted. He was furious because Little Lamb hadn't come.

"Oh, so *you* are Wolfgang?" cried Mama Sheep in shock.

"Got a problem with that?" snarled Wolf. "If you weren't so old and tough, why I'd . . ."

This was all too much for the old, gray dog. "Quiet!" he cried. "Or I'll fetch the police!"

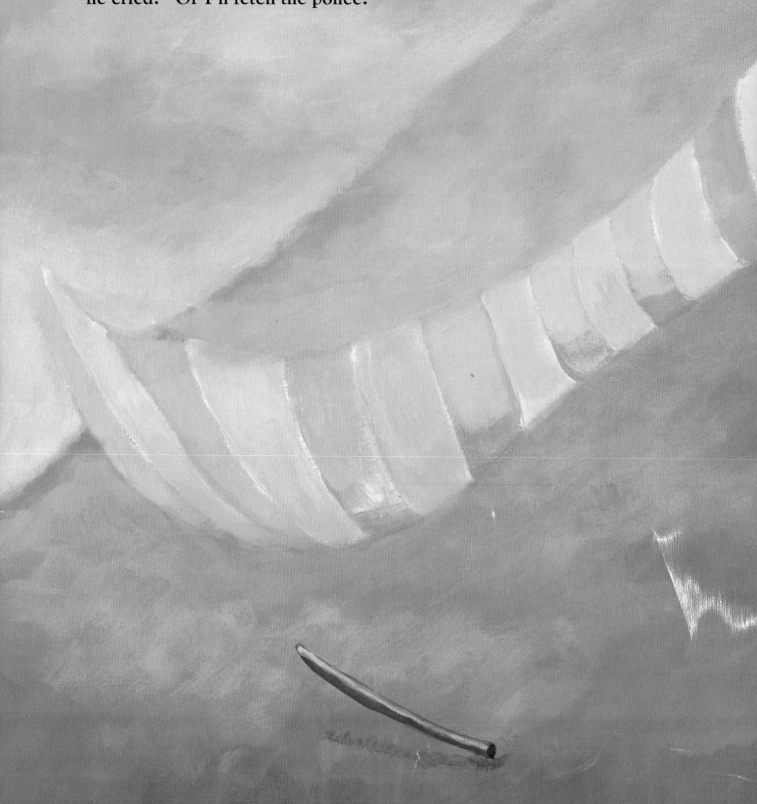

Mama Sheep was not quiet, however.

"I want to know what's going on, this instant! Why do you keep writing my child those letters?"

"Well now, ahem . . . I, ah, ah . . ." stammered Wolfgang.

Mama Sheep smelled trouble. "I don't know exactly what you are up to, but you are going to write a letter to my Little Lamb at once, and it's going to be a good-bye letter," she said angrily.

Mama Sheep dictated:

Dear Little Lamb,

Unfortunately, I'm very busy right now. Must study the moon and count woolly clouds. Alas—I have no more time to write letters.

Sincerely,
Wolfgang, your former friend

"Oh, but he was such a good friend," sniffled Little Lamb. "When I'm bigger, I'll send him a huge packet of sausages!"

"Oh, sure," said Papa Sheep, "someday, when you are bigger. Much bigger."

"Wolfgang was going to tell me all about Australia, and the tender grass, and all the sheep that live there," Little Lamb bleated sadly.

"Moving might not be such a bad idea, Papa," said Mama Sheep, handing her husband a map of Australia.

"Maybe I could find a new friend there, a sheep friend!" Little Lamb said, starting to cheer up.

"Oh, a small, tender, fluffy lamb like you will find many friends there," said Mama Sheep.

"Great!" cried Little Lamb. "Let's go!"

Wolf stood high up on the mountain, peering through his telescope. And what did he see?

A small, white, fluffy thing boarding a bus to Australia.

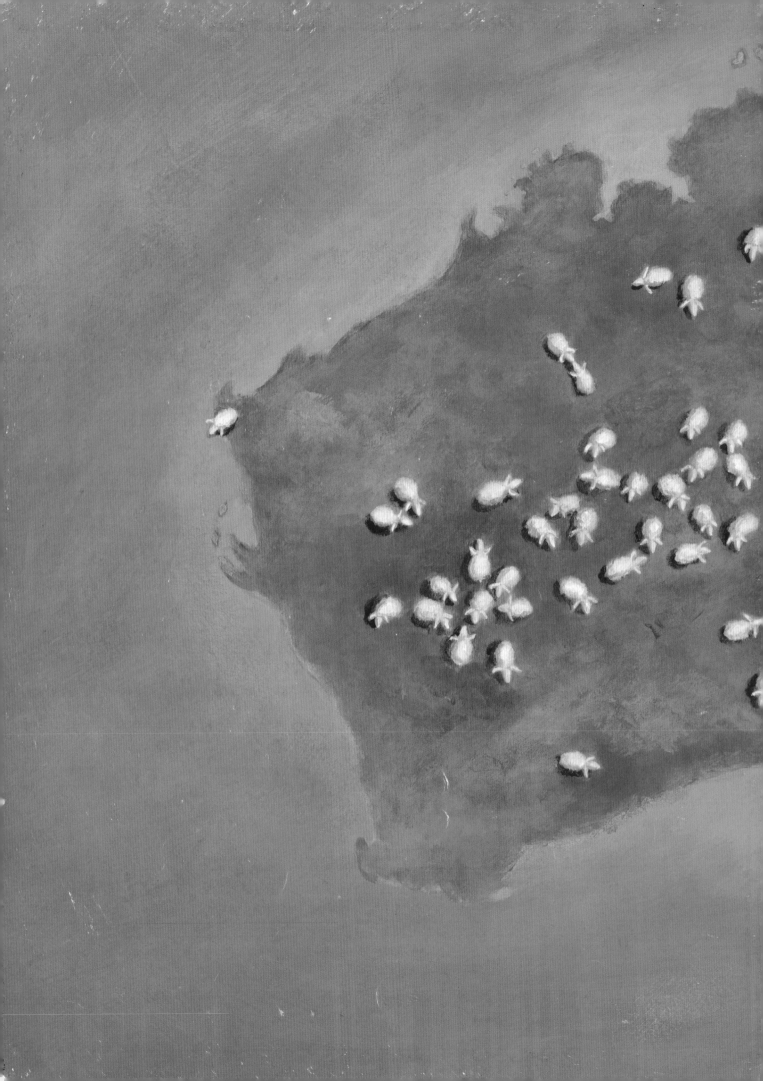